BETWEEN FRIENDS
ENTRE AMIGOS

Written by Juliana Anthony Hernández and Elena Gaona
Illustrations by Ely Ely

BETWEEN FRIENDS
ENTRE AMIGOS

La Joya Press
Published by La Joya Press, LLC
La Jolla, CA

Text set in Gochi Hand.

Library of Congress Cataloging-in-Publication Data
LCCN 2021913220
Anthony Hernández, Juliana
Gaona, Elena
Between Friends / Entre Amigos / by Juliana Anthony Hernández
and Elena Gaona / Illustrations by Ely Ely.

Summary: A bilingual book of words and images on friendship.
ISBN 978-1-7374651-0-2 (Hardcover)
ISBN 978-1-7374651-1-9 (Paperback)
Bilingual, Friendship

Authors: Juliana Anthony Hernández and Elena Gaona
Illustrator: Melissa Zúñiga (Ely Ely)
Designer: María Estela González Acevedo
Spanish Editor: Sandra Reyes Carrillo

Publisher's Cataloging-in-Publication data

Names: Hernandez, Juliana Anthony, author. | Gaona, Elena, author. | Zuniga, Melissa, illustrator.
Title: Entre amigos / Between friends / by Juliana Anthony Hernandez and Elena Gaona;
illustrated by Melissa Zuniga.
Description: San Diego, CA: La Joya Press, 2022. | Summary: Between Friends is a bilingual book about fun, silly,
true friends who can make life sweeter.
Identifiers: LCCN: 2021913220 | HARDCOVER ISBN: 978-1-7374651-0-2 | PAPERBACK ISBN 978-1-7374651-1-9
Subjects: LCSH Friendship--Juvenile literature. | Bilingual materials.
| BISAC JUVENILE NONFICTION / Social Topics / Friendship
Classification: LCC BF575.F66 H47 2022 | DDC 177.62--dc23

For Derek, my boys George, Julián and Tomás, mis padres Hermila
y Juan, my brothers Macario y Chinto, mi prima Laura,
my BFF Elena y amigas Zulma, Rosa, Marybeth, Juanita, Vivi,
Quitze, Maricielo, Tye, Laura, Laurie, Miri y Cindy.
Journey through life with great friends!
¡Viaja por la vida con grandes amigos!
J.A.H.

***

For Keith, Maya and Fabi, Mami y Papi, Max, Ricardo,
my BFF Juli who allowed me to come on this adventure, and Mari,
Cecy, Rasheea, Liz, Jen, Monika, Marcy, Vivi and Christina.
M.E.G.

***

To/Para:

From/De:

_____

_____

_____

Kindness

Between friends, there is kindness.
A friend can be there for you
when you're sad and help
you get up when you fall.

Amabilidad

Entre amigos, somos amables.
Un amigo puede estar para ti
cuando te sientes triste, y te
ayuda a levantarte si te caes.

Support

Between friends, there is support.
Friends love watching you shine and
cheering you on!

Apoyo

Entre amigos, nos apoyamos.
¡A tus amigos les encanta verte brillar
y aplaudirte!

Help

Between friends, there is help.
When your work piles up,
a good friend can be there!

Ayuda

Entre amigos, nos ayudamos.
¡Cuando tienes mucho trabajo,
un buen amigo te puede ayudar!

Love

Between friends, there is love.
Some friends open their hearts
to you.

Amor

Entre amigos, hay amor.
Hay amigos que te comparten
su corazón.

Respect

Between friends, there is respect.
Friends try to think about your feelings
and your personal space.

Respeto

Entre amigos, hay respeto.
Los amigos tratan de pensar en tus
sentimientos y en tu espacio personal.

Laughter

Between friends, there are lots of laughs.
Some friends make you giggle, which
makes you feel happy—like the sun
is shining down on you.

Risas

Entre amigos, hay muchas risas.
Existen amigos que te hacen reír
y eso te pone feliz, como si el sol
brillara sobre ti.

Be Yourself

Between friends, we are open and real.
Friends will listen to your fears
and feelings, big or small, and will let
you be yourself.

Sé tú mismo

Entre amigos, somos sinceros y reales.
Los amigos escucharán tus miedos
y sentimientos, sean grandes o pequeños,
y te dejarán ser tú mismo.

Comfortable

Between friends, we feel comfortable.
Some friends know you so well
that they can tell when you need
to do a happy dance!

Cómodas

Entre amigas, nos sentimos cómodas.
Algunas amigas te conocen tan bien
que saben cuándo necesitas
bailar de alegría.

Fun

Between friends, there is fun.
Some friends encourage you to go on fun adventures
that you have never experienced before.

Diversión

Entre amigos, hay diversión.
Hay amigos que pueden animarte
a vivir nuevas aventuras divertidas.

Listen

Between friends, we listen.
Friends love listening to your jokes,
stories, thoughts, and opinions.

Escuchar

Entre amigos, nos escuchamos.
A tus amigos les encanta escuchar tus chistes,
historias, pensamientos y opiniones.

caring

Between friends, there is caring.
A friend will try to protect you
when it matters.

cuidado

Entre amigos, nos cuidamos.
Una amiga intentará protegerte
cuando sea necesario.

Trust

Between friends, there is trust.
Friends believe in you! They say, "I can count
on you, and you can count on me!"

Confianza

Entre amigas, hay confianza.
Las amigas creen en ti. Dicen, "¡Puedo contar
contigo y tú puedes contar conmigo!"

Forgiveness

Between friends, there is forgiveness.
Friends can make mistakes. Talking about a
disagreement can be a great way to solve it.

Perdón

Entre amigos, existe el perdón.
Los amigos pueden cometer errores. Hablar sobre
un desacuerdo puede ayudar a resolverlo.

Diversity

Between friends, we're all different. It feels good to have friends who love and accept all the ways you are unique and different. Diversity makes friendship more special—and everyone's days more fun!

Diversidad

Entre amigos, somos todos diferentes. Es bonito tener amigos que nos quieren y que aceptan todas las formas en las que somos únicos y diferentes. La diversidad hace la amistad más especial y los días más divertidos.

Honesty

Between friends, we are honest.
A friend will always try to tell the truth about
their actions and feelings, even if it's hard.

Honestidad

Entre amigos, somos honestos.
Un amigo intentará siempre decir la verdad sobre
sus acciones y sentimientos, incluso cuando sea difícil.

Friends
◆◆◆
Amigos

Between friends, we can help
each other feel appreciated,
healthy, and happy.
A good friend will make life
sweeter by supporting you
during the sad times and by
being there to celebrate the
good times! As I often say,
"I'm so grateful to be among
friends!"

Entre amigos nos podemos ayudar a sentir apreciados, sanos y felices.
¡Un buen amigo te hará la vida más dulce apoyándote durante los momentos tristes y también estará ahí para celebrar los momentos felices! Como suelo decir: "¡Estoy agradecido de estar entre amigos!"

About the Authors and Illustrator
Acerca de las autoras e ilustradora

Juliana Hernández M.Ed. grew up in the Oak Cliff neighborhood of Dallas, TX, in a Mexican-American family. They would visit family in Mexico every summer, and she continued her love of travel by taking trips throughout the world and learning about different cultures. She received her bachelor's degree from Texas Woman's University and a master's in education from Texas A&M Commerce. Juliana loves being a bilingual educator and a mother. She now lives in La Jolla, California with her husband Derek and their three sons. During her free time, she enjoys traveling, hiking, the beach, volunteering with the San Diego Symphony and entertaining family and friends.

Juliana Hernández creció en el vecindario de Oak Cliff en Dallas, TX, en una familia mexicoamericana. Visitaban a su familia en México todos los veranos, y ella continuó con su amor por los viajes al viajar por todo el mundo y aprender sobre diferentes culturas. Recibió su licenciatura de la Texas Woman's University y una maestría en Educación de la Texas A&M Commerce. Le gusta mucho ser madre y educadora bilingüe. Juliana ahora vive en La Jolla, California, con su esposo Derek y sus tres hijos. Durante su tiempo libre le gusta viajar, hacer caminatas, ir a la playa, ser voluntaria con la Sinfonía de San Diego y disfrutar tiempo con su familia y amigos.

Elena Gaona is a bilingual communicator who has focused on issues of equity and representation. She grew up in a Mexican immigrant family home in Dallas, Texas. She was a newspaper reporter covering everything from immigration to higher education, culture and business; followed by communication roles at nonprofits and government agencies in Washington, DC. She and her spouse Keith have two daughters. When she has free time, she blogs about Latinos in DC, writes stories and throws parties.

Elena Gaona es una comunicadora bilingüe que se ha enfocado en temas de equidad y representación. Creció en una familia de inmigrantes mexicanos en Dallas, Texas. Era reportera de periódicos y cubría de todo, desde inmigración y educación superior, hasta cultura y negocios; seguido por roles de comunicación en organizaciones sin fines de lucro y agencias gubernamentales en Washington, DC. Ella y su esposo Keith tienen dos hijas. Cuando tiene tiempo libre, escribe blogs sobre la comunidad latina en DC, escribe historias y organiza fiestas.

Melissa Zúñiga, better known as Ely Ely, is a Mexican illustrator from Aguascalientes who currently lives in Mexico City. After finishing her studies in graphic design, she worked for a few years in various marketing agencies while also doing freelance work as an illustrator and mural painter, then launched her own illustration studio six years ago. Women, Mexican graphical elements, nature, and color are the basis for her creativity and inspiration, and these things can frequently be found in her illustrations, murals, and other work. She has worked on numerous projects in Mexico and abroad, including partnerships with Disney, Google, MaryKay, Maybelline, Clinique, Dole Sunshine, Danone, and Bonafont, among others.

Melissa Zúñiga, mejor conocida como Ely Ely, es una ilustradora mexicana originaria de Aguascalientes que actualmente reside en Ciudad de México. Estudió Diseño Gráfico, y después de trabajar un par de años en agencias de publicidad y a la par hacer proyectos de ilustración y muralismo, fundó su propio estudio de ilustración. Las mujeres, la gráfica mexicana, la naturaleza y el color son parte fundamental de su creatividad e inspiración, y frecuentemente se ven plasmados en sus ilustraciones, productos y murales. Ha trabajado en diferentes proyectos dentro y fuera de México, incluyendo colaboraciones con Disney, Google, MaryKay, Maybelline, Clinique, Dole Sunshine, Danone y Bonafont, entre otras.

Acknowledgements
We'd like to thank clinical psychologist Mariana Icazbalceta de la Peña, Dr. Kesha Gilmore, and Dr. Ana Laura, Regina and Octavio Gaona, and Adriana Gaona, for helping us make this book better.

Agradecimientos
Queremos agradecer a la Psicóloga Clínica Mariana Icazbalceta de la Peña, a la Dra. Kesha Gilmore y a la Dra. Ana Laura, Regina y Lic. Octavio Gaona, y a Adriana Gaona, por ayudarnos a mejorar este libro.

www.lajoyapress.com

Made in the USA
Middletown, DE
07 August 2022

70421327R00022